Herbie Br

Eddie the Duck

Illustrated by Ann Kronheimer

PUFFIN BOOKS

For Jacks

PUFFIN BOOKS

Published by the Penguin Group
Penguin Books Ltd, 27 Wrights Lane, London W8 5TZ, England
Penguin Putnam Inc., 375 Hudson Street, New York, New York 10014, USA
Penguin Books Australia Ltd, Ringwood, Victoria, Australia
Penguin Books Canada Ltd, 10 Alcorn Avenue, Toronto, Ontario, Canada M4V 3B2
Penguin Books (NZ) Ltd, 182–190 Wairau Road, Auckland 10, New Zealand

Penguin Books Ltd, Registered Offices: Harmondsworth, Middlesex, England

First published 1998
3 5 7 9 10 8 6 4

Text copyright © Herbie Brennan, 1998
Illustrations copyright © Ann Kronheimer, 1998
All rights reserved

The moral right of the author and illustrator has been asserted

Typeset in Times New Roman Schoolbook

Printed in Hong Kong by Midas Printing Limited

British Library Cataloguing in Publication Data
A CIP catalogue record for this book is available from the British Library

ISBN 0–140–38632–7

··· Contents ···

"Mad Duck Stole My Trousers," Says Old-age Pensioner

Bedfordshire Times, 24 June 1994

1. Duck in the City

My name is Eddie. I'm a duck.
It was night in the city. I
was out waddling the dog and
wondering what to do with my life.
Suddenly an alarm sounded. I
turned to look and the dog ran off.
But that was the least of my
worries.

The alarm was ringing outside the First National Bank. Beneath it was a notice. The notice said CLOSED.

Through the window I could see masked men. Right up against the pavement was a black car with its engine running.

This didn't look good.

I wondered if I should call the cops. Or maybe quack for help. But who listens to a duck?

Just then, seventeen police cars screeched around the corner, sirens blaring. In seconds, cops were everywhere.

A burly sergeant with a crew-cut shouted through a loud hailer, "You are surrounded. Come out with your hands up!"

The bank door crashed open. Masked men piled out. One of them grabbed me.

"Back off or the duck gets it!" he called back.

I had just time to notice the cops backing off before I was bundled into the black car. "Hang on to him, Marvin," the man ordered.

The car drove away in a cloud of garlic. There was a big guy with a mask to my right. There was a big guy with a mask to my left. They both pulled off their masks and grinned at me nastily.

I sank back in the leather seat with a sigh. There was no doubt about it. I'd been ducknapped!

2. Duck in a Car

The car screamed through the city. I glanced through the back window. The cops were following, but at a distance.

"You'll never get away with this!" I said.

"Shut your beak," said the big

guy on the right and stuck his
Mark Two splurge gun in my face.
I shut it.

The car swung right, then left. It
raced down an alley, sending
cardboard boxes flying.

Then we were in Chinatown,
knocking down the fast-food stalls.
Chinamen shook their fists at us,
but the big guys didn't care. They
were tough cookies.

I glanced through the back
window again. The police cars
were nowhere in sight. I was on
my own.

The car got on the bridge out of
town and I knew I was in big
trouble. Once they left the city they
could hide out anywhere.

But it turned out they weren't leaving the city at all. They were on the bridge for a different reason.

Suddenly, I wondered what they planned to do with me. Keep me as a hostage? Hold me for ransom? Somehow I didn't think so. The car bulged with sacks of money from the bank.

They needed a ransom like I needed
separate toes.

As if he was reading my
thoughts, the driver said, "What we
going to do with the duck, Dan?"

The big guy on my left said,
"This bird can identify us now,
Harold. We gotta rub him out!"

3. Duck in the Water

They knotted a spotted hanky round my eyes and tied my wings behind my back.

Then they threw me over the bridge.

Boy, were those guys idiots! They tried to drown a *duck*?

I hit the water paddling and
shook the hanky off my head. My
wings were still tied, but I didn't
need them. I started down the river
like a power boat.

14

About this time, the guys on the
bridge noticed what was happening.
   "Hey, he's getting away!"
shouted the driver.
   I glanced back to see them

levelling their splurge guns. It gave me some encouragement to paddle faster.

SPLAT! A stinging jet of purple yuck splurged past my ear.

SPLAT! SPLAT! SPLAT! Then another and another.

I wove from side to side to make a tougher target. Nobody takes a purple duck seriously.

SPLAT! SPLAT!

QUACK! QUACK!

One of the guys on the bridge was blowing a duck lure. It sounded like another duck that needed help.

I wasn't falling for that old trick.

Still paddling, I turned a corner in the river and dived into the reeds. They'd never find me now. I was safe.

Or so I thought.

4. Duck under Fire

I climbed out of the water shivering and managed to get the ropes off my wings. I was pretty mad at the robbers. They'd grabbed me, threatened me, tried to kill me and made me lose my dog. I needed to get even.

But first I needed a disguise.

I shook the water off my feathers. Then I crept towards the row of waterfront houses behind me.

It was dark here away from the street lights so I thought no one would see me.

In the back yard of one of the houses, somebody had left their washing on the line all night. There was a shirt, a set of long johns and a pair of trousers.

I felt the clothing carefully. The
long johns were still wet but the
shirt and trousers were dry. They
were both too big for me, but they
would have to do. I tugged the
trousers off the line.

I was just pulling them up when
a light went on and an upstairs
window slammed open. An old coot
stuck his head out.

"What do you think you're
doing, duck?" he shouted.

"Waiting for a bus," I wise-quacked.

A boot came sailing out of the window. The old coot's aim was pretty good. I took off out of his back yard like a scalded cat.

That was something else the bank robbers were going to have to pay for.

5. Ducking and Diving

I figured when you're looking for lowlife, you have to start by talking to lowlife. So I went into a low dive off the pier.

The place was full of smoke and sailors. I'd bought a hat, shoes and

shades to go with the old coot's
trousers, so nobody recognized me.

I waddled up to the bar. "Gimme
a glass of swamp water," I said out
of the side of my beak. The barman
turned away in disgust.

A cool blonde sidled up. "Want some company, big boy?" she asked.

I sniffed, which isn't easy for a duck. "Not unless you know a gorilla called Dan who hangs around with a goon named Marvin," I said.

There was a sudden silence in the bar. Sailors started to edge away from me. A little guy with a face like a rat left hurriedly by the back door. The barman dropped a glass.

But the blonde played it cool. "What's it worth to you?" she asked.

"A free course of swimming lessons and all the eggs you can eat," I said.

"This Dan and Marvin," said the blonde, "they wouldn't be teamed up with a character called Harold, by any chance?"

I'd struck lucky. Harold was the name of the driver. I nodded, my beak suddenly dry with excitement.

The blonde smiled. "Buy me a drink, baby, and I'll tell you all about it."

6. Duck on the Roof

The blonde's name was Gloria La Rue. What she told me sent me off to a seedy part of town. I ate the seeds gratefully. It was my first decent meal all day.

Then I questioned a bag lady,

the leader of a street gang and the
cop on the beat. They all told me
the same thing. Three scumbags
named Harold, Dan and Marvin
ran a garlic-packing business down
in dockland.

I decided to make it my next

port of call. On the way I bought
an evening paper. The big story
said the Mayor was offering a half
a million reward for the capture of
the robbers. That money had my
name on it.

It was a fine night, raining hard.

The dockland streets were wet and empty. At the end of a narrow alley, I saw a sign. It said:

HAROLD, DAN AND MARVIN'S GARLIC-PACKING BUSINESS

I figured this must be the place.

I also figured it would be bad news to use the front door, so I climbed the fire escape on to the roof. As I looked across the skyline, I felt a sudden twinge. This was my city.

But it was no time for sentiment. I could see a bright glow streaming from a skylight. I went across and peered through the filthy glass.

It was the correct place all right.

The three goons who ducknapped
me were down below packing
cardboard boxes on a big conveyor
belt.

Only it wasn't garlic they were packing. It was money stolen from the bank. I leaned forward to get a better look, lost my balance and crashed right through the skylight in a shower of glass.

I was so surprised, I forgot how to fly.

7. Duck in Trouble

T he three goons looked up.
"Duck!" shouted Marvin when
he saw me.

Dan and Harold both ducked
and hit their heads on the conveyor
belt. Their eyes turned up. They

spun round twice, then fell back like they were hit by a number nine bus.

That was two less goons to worry about, but I still had problems. I landed right in one of the cardboard boxes on the conveyor belt. It was half full of

money which broke my fall, but the whole thing left me a little dazed.

I preened my feathers and shook my head to clear it. Then I saw the box was being carried towards two huge robot arms that reached out to grab it.

I watched wide-eyed, wondering if I was going quackers. But this was no mistake. The arms belonged to a machine that grabbed boxes, closed them up and sealed them with sticky tape.

If I didn't move fast, that was exactly what was going to happen to my box – with me inside.

The machine had grabbed the box ahead of me by the time I got my head together. But then I exploded into action.

I jumped out of my box in a cloud of cash and feathers. The robot arms reached out and grabbed. The box was sealed and stacked in half a second, but not with me inside.

I might have heaved a sigh of relief except for one thing. I was still in big trouble.

8. Duck-in-a-box?

When I jumped, I landed on the conveyor belt three boxes down. By this stage I'd remembered how to fly, but now my foot was caught so I couldn't take off.

The conveyor belt carried me towards the robot arms. Just three

boxes to go, then me. Once I
hit that machine I'd be wrapped
and sealed and stacked up
helpless.

The arms grabbed the first box.
Close, tape, seal, stack.

I struggled to free my foot. It
was jammed between the rollers of
the conveyor belt.

The arms grabbed the second
box. *Close, tape, seal, stack.*

I twisted and pulled, struggled
and jerked. I flapped my wings and
squawked with fright. What I didn't
do was free the foot.

The arms grabbed the third box.
Close, tape, seal, stack.

There was nothing between me
and the machine now.

Just seconds left before I
was closed, taped, sealed and
stacked. After that it was only
a matter of time before Marvin
woke up Dan and Harold

and the three goons came to get
me.

Then I remembered. I was
wearing shoes.

I started to pull at the laces.

The robot arms were reaching out for me as they came loose. I jerked my foot out of the shoe and jumped sideways, wings flapping.

The machine grabbed thin air. I was safe.

But not for long.

9. Duck on Top

Before I could catch my breath,
I heard running footsteps. I
looked over my shoulder. Marvin
was bearing down on me like
rolling thunder.

"This is the end of you, Duck!"
he cried.

I took off down the rows of boxes. In this part of the warehouse, the ceiling was too low to fly.

Marvin came after me, hurling abuse.

I ducked round a corner, but he spotted me and followed.

"I'm going to serve you up with green peas!" he shouted.

I turned another corner, raced down the row, then spotted a door marked EXIT. I flew at it, but it was locked.

"Your goose is cooked, Duck!" Marvin shouted. "I got you now!"

I dived between his legs and for
a minute I thought I'd made it free.
But Marvin came after me again. I
scuttled back between the stacked-
up boxes.

In seconds I was back at the
conveyor belt. Marvin was right
behind me. There was only one
thing for it. Low ceiling or not, I
flew.

Marvin made a dive to grab me and fell full length on the conveyor belt.

"Yipes!" he yelled as I circled back above his head.

It was his last word on the matter. The robot arms grabbed him, folded him in half, then wrapped him up with tape and stacked him.

I checked the other two were still unconscious. Then I called the cops.

10. Duck in Gravy

The Mayor made a pretty speech. Stuff about me being an example to the whole community.

Then he handed over the reward.

You can buy a lot of birdseed with half a million smackers.

But I already knew how I
planned to spend it.

I went right round to my new
office. Gloria La Rue was sitting on
the reception desk polishing her
nails.

"Hi, boss," she said. "Your dog
came back."

"Thanks, babe," I said.

I sailed my hat towards the
hatstand. At last I knew what I
wanted to do with my life. This was

it. The world's first Private Ducktective Agency.

I swanned into my private office and kicked shut the door.